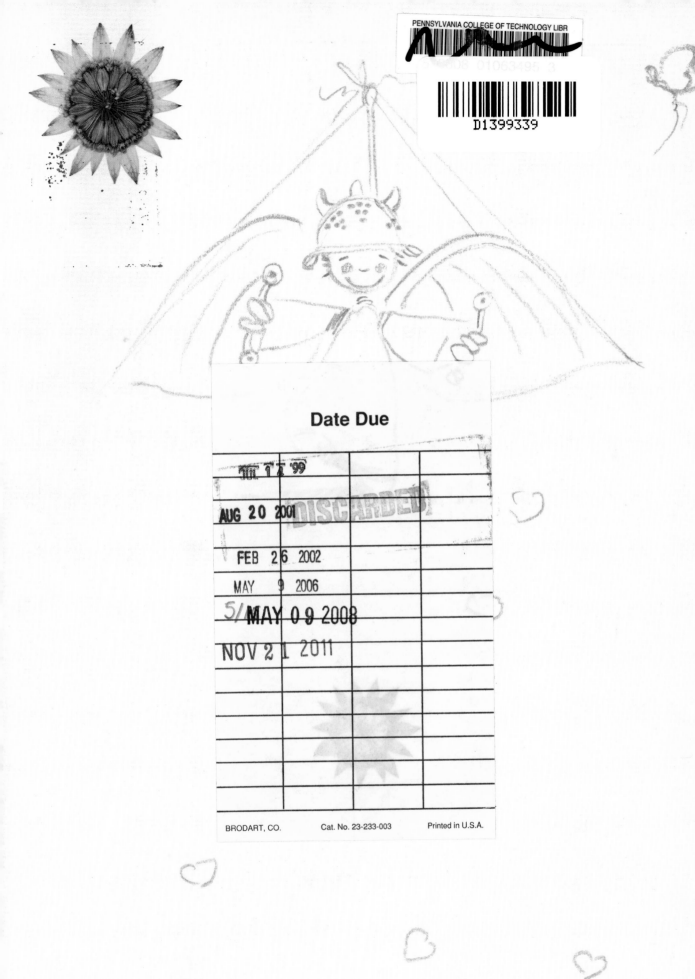

Date Due

First published in the United States, Great Britain, Canada, Australia,
and New Zealand in 1994 by North-South Books, an imprint of
Nord-Süd Verlag AG, Gossau Zürich, Switzerland.

Distributed in the United States by North-South Books Inc., New York.

Library of Congress Cataloging-in-Publication Data is available.
A CIP catalogue record for this book is available from The British Library.
ISBN 1-55858-306-8 (TRADE BINDING)
ISBN 1-55858-307-6 (LIBRARY BINDING)

10 9 8 7 6 5 4 3 2 1
Printed in Belgium

DOMINIQUE FALDA

NIGHT
FLIGHT

TRANSLATED
BY J. ALISON JAMES

NORTH-SOUTH BOOKS

NEW YORK / LONDON

Julian loved the night.
He loved to sit with his two companions, the bird and the cat,
and watch the moon move across the sky.

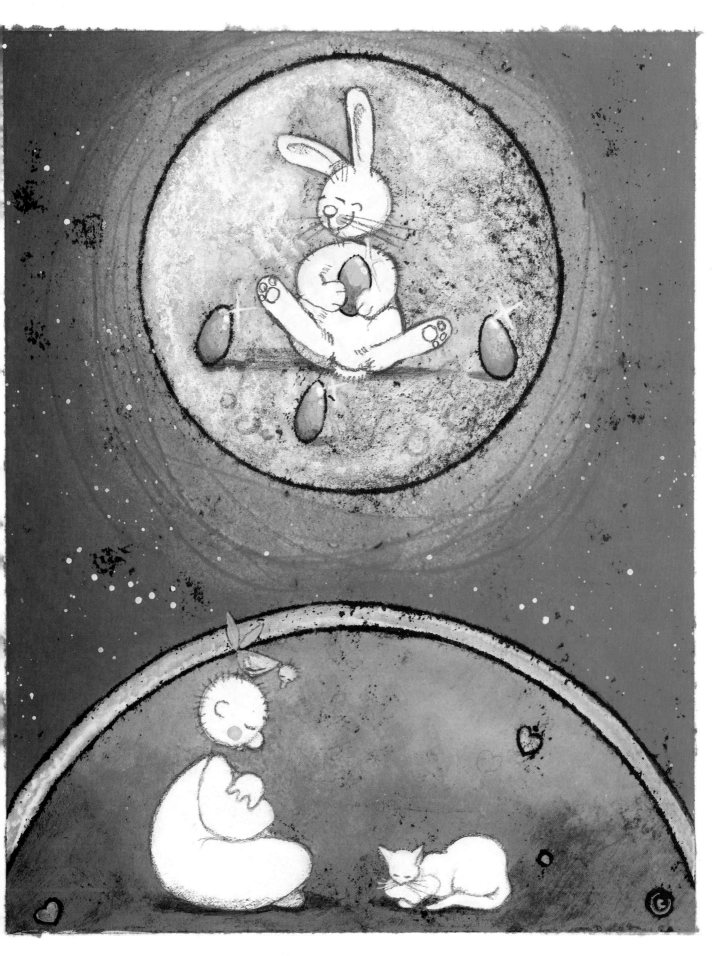

One night Julian thought he saw a rabbit playing with
her golden eggs in the mottled shadows of the moon.
May I come and play with you?" Julian wanted to know.

The rabbit seemed welcoming. So Julian built a ladder,
taller than the tallest tree, and climbed into the sky.
But he was nowhere near the moon.

"I'll have to fly," Julian decided. "But how? I have no wings."
 He inspected the bird and thought and thought.
"I know," he said. "I'll invent a machine."

He scribbled furiously in a notebook. He filled up hundreds
of pages. He thought about air, and the shape of a wing.
Finally he had it. A flying machine!

'I'll float like a feather, and I'll fly up in the sky
and play with the eggs of the Rabbit in the Moon."
The bird was bewildered. The cat was amused.

"Hooray! Hooray! Up…up…and away!" cried Julian
as he launched himself into the air.
"Here I come, Rabbit. Look at meeeee! *Uh-oh…*"

BOOM! Julian landed in the grass.
His wings were torn. His clothes were a mess.
"My wings don't work," he said to the bird.

He bandaged his wounds, picked up his pen,
and opened his notebook again.
He contemplated structure and weight and force until…

suddenly he saw something astonishing.
The great Bullabou, coming home from the fair,
with a balloon in the shape of a rabbit.

Balloon. Rabbit. Rabbit balloon. Rabbit in the Moon.
've got it!" Julian shouted, and he bounced for joy.

Julian volunteered the cat as a test pilot.
"Meow!" howled the frightened cat.
But Julian was thrilled. "It works! It really works!"

So he built   a flying ship
from balsa wood and paint and glue,
with feathers on the oars.

Then gently rocking, up he flew
into the rumbling, thundering night,
up to his friend the Rabbit in the Moon.

Suddenly he was shocked by a spike of lightning—

and he slipped from the sky, spinning faster and faster,
down to the earth, where he belonged.
The moon was no friend to him.

Julian lay in the grass, stunned and hurt and lonely.
He thought maybe he had died.
His eyes were closed. His breath was still.

Then soft hands picked up his head
and warm tears watered his cheeks
and dripped down his nose, and tickled—

ATCHOOO! sneezed Julian, and he opened his eyes.

The world was spinning, the stars were singing,
the Rabbit in the Moon was dancing for joy.
Was Julian crazy? Was he in trouble? No! He was in…

LOVE!

Julian and Josie, best of friends,
walked hand in hand across the clover
and watched the morning-glory sun come up.

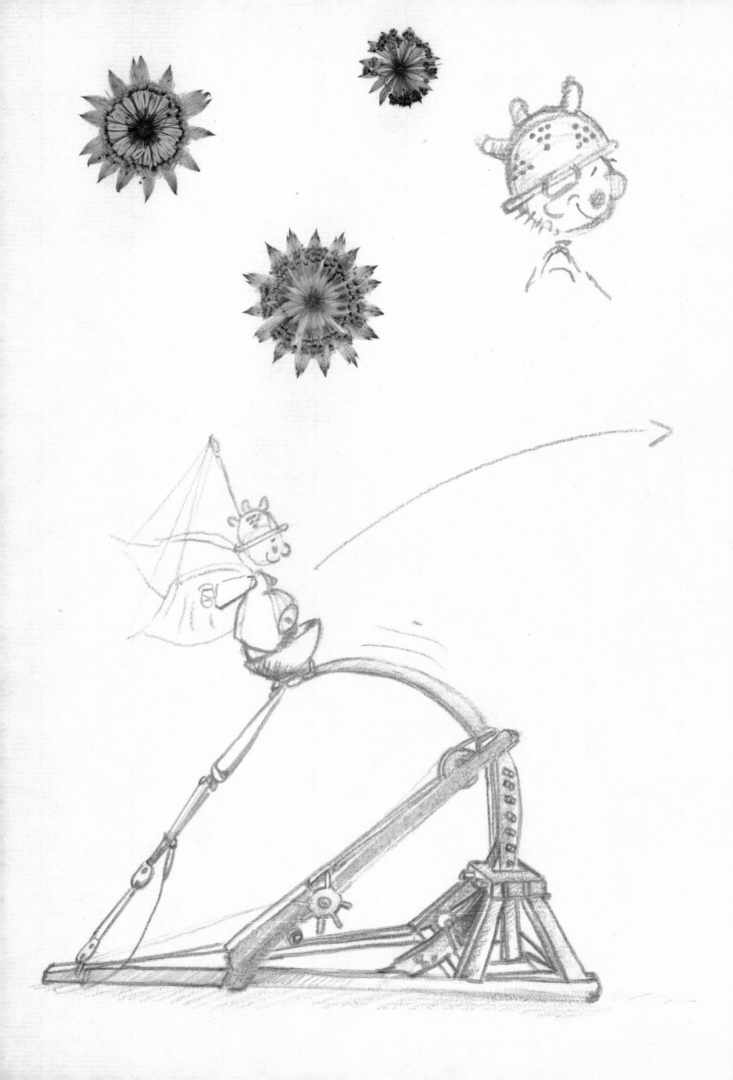